The Animals Who Woke Up for
CHRISTMAS

Stella Ormai

HAPPY HOUSE BOOKS
Random House, Inc.

Winter is coming!" announced Snowshoe Hare as a cold frosty wind blew through North Woods one day.

Tubby Mole looked at the bare bushes beside the path and yawned loudly. "Ahhhh…I'm ready to sleep," he said. "As soon as all the blackberries are gone, I know it's time to hibernate."

Not far away the three little Raccoon children—Fil, Bert, and Hazel—were tumbling in a pile of dead leaves. They were laughing and shouting and paying no attention to the frosty wind.

"Foolish children," grumbled Mrs. Shrew as she picked up an acorn the wind had knocked to the ground. "They should be storing food in their nest—not playing noisy games!"

Suddenly the air was full of bird song and the sound of flapping wings. A flock of sparrows stopped to rest on the branches of an oak tree.

Mrs. Shrew frowned and looked up. "What are you so chirpy about?" she said. "Don't you know that winter is coming and it's almost time to hibernate?"

The birds stared down at the animals on the ground.

"Don't you know that it's time to fly south to a warmer place?" asked Mrs. Sparrow.

"Fly? Hah!" snapped Mrs. Shrew. "That's easy for birds to say! But we furry animals have to stay right here in cold North Woods. That's why we go to sleep until spring."

Mrs. Sparrow cocked her head thoughtfully. "But...if you are asleep all winter, you will miss Christmas."

Just then three little raccoon heads popped out of the leaves. "What's Christmas?" cried Fil, Bert, and Hazel.

"Well, I'm sure it has nothing to do with us," muttered Mrs. Shrew, and she stuffed a few more acorns into her bundle.

"I've heard of Christmas," said Brownie Bear, who had just come up the path with Old Groundhog. "But I don't know much about it."

So Mrs. Sparrow tried to describe Christmas to the furry animals who had gathered below the oak tree.

"It's a wonderful time of year," she began. "We are all together. We decorate a fir tree. We eat delicious treats. We sing Christmas songs. We give one another presents."

"Presents!" cried the Raccoon children. "We want Christmas too."

"Treats!" exclaimed Tubby Mole with a grin.

"And songs!" added Brownie Bear.

"Hmmmmm," said Snowshoe Hare. "I wonder if we couldn't have Christmas right here in North Woods."

"Christmas can be anywhere," called Mrs. Sparrow as she and the other birds flew away.

"Hooray!" the animals shouted. And before Mrs. Shrew could pick up another acorn, they began making preparations.

First the animals decided that they would celebrate Christmas in Brownie Bear's cave, because he had the biggest house. Brownie began to decorate. He hung up pine branches and pine cones and even some mistletoe.

Snowshoe chopped down a fir tree and took it to Brownie's cave.

Fil, Bert, and Hazel made decorations for the tree.

Tubby Mole baked wild plum pudding and chestnut pie and blackberry cake.

Old Groundhog brewed a big batch of snappy root beer.

Even cranky Mrs. Shrew thought of something to do. She made dozens and dozens of tiny candles out of beeswax.

But the best preparations of all were done in secret. Everyone disappeared now and then to make presents!

By and by the animals were ready for Christmas,
but Christmas had not come to North Woods. And
it was getting colder and colder. The frosty air made
everyone shiver.

"We must stay underground in our warm beds," said
Snowshoe, pulling his woolly scarf tighter.

"But what if we go to sleep?" asked Tubby. "How will we
wake up for Christmas?"

They had all been so busy getting ready for Christmas,
no one had thought about *this*!

"All that work for nothing!" said Mrs. Shrew. "As soon
as we're asleep, there is nothing that can wake us up except
the warm air of spring."

Suddenly the merry voice of Reddy Cardinal sang out. "Hello...can I help? I'm awake all winter. I promise to wake you on Christmas day."

"That's perfect!" said Snowshoe. "Now we can have Christmas in North Woods."

And so the animals of North Woods snuggled into their
beds and went to sleep—
Snowshoe in his rabbit hole,
Old Groundhog in his burrow,
Mrs. Shrew in her little nest,
Brownie Bear in his big cave,
Tubby Mole in his underground tunnel,
and Fil, Bert, and Hazel in their hollow tree.

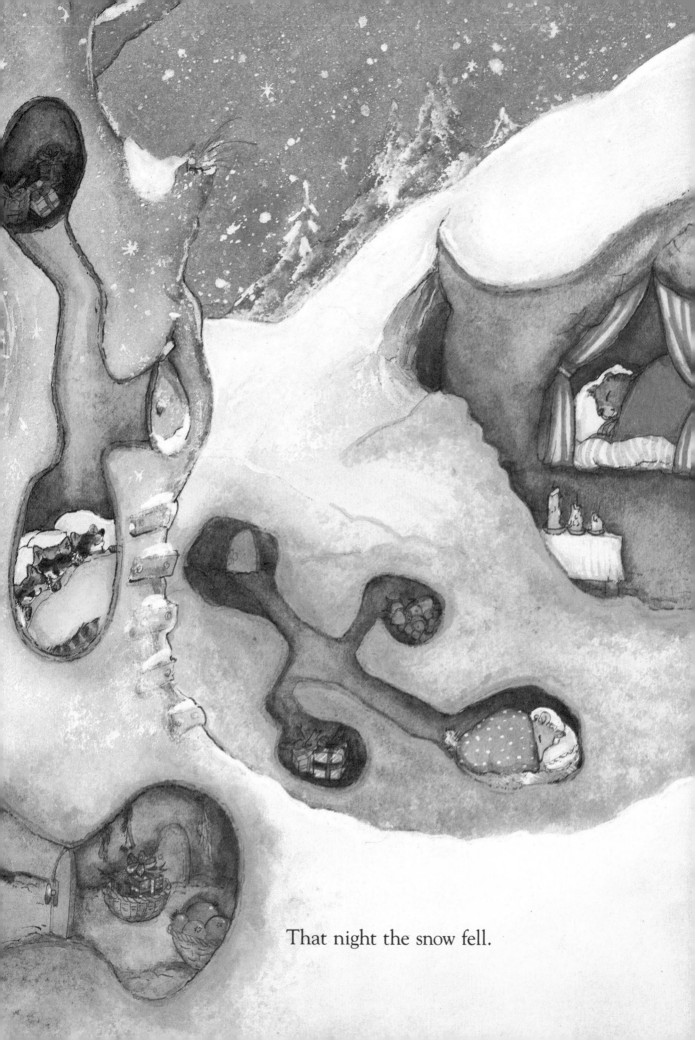

That night the snow fell.

Many weeks went by. Winter came. Then one morning a fresh new snow fell and it whispered *Christmas...Christmas...* Reddy Cardinal remembered his promise.

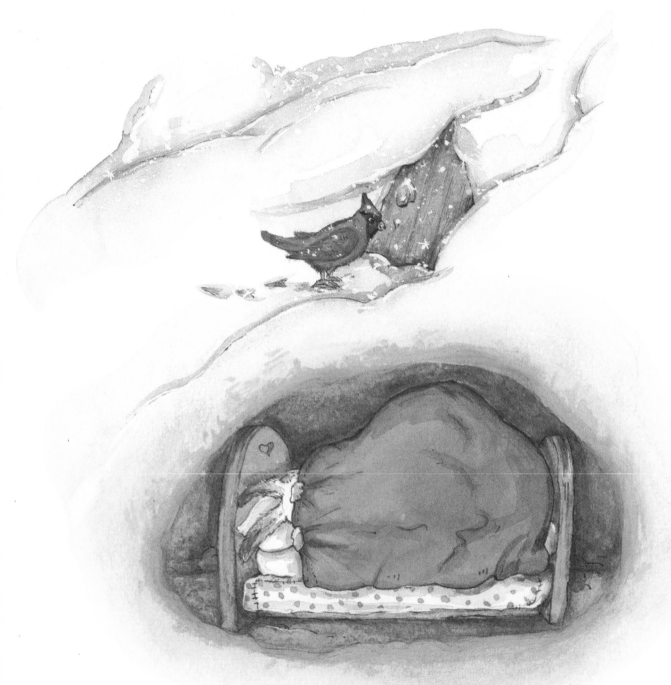

He flew down and tapped on Snowshoe's door. "Wake up! It's Christmas!" he chirped.

Snowshoe rolled over in his sleep and pulled the covers over his ears. He did not wake up.

Reddy went from door to door. "Wake up! Wake up! It's Christmas!" he called.

"I'm sleeping!"
answered Tubby Mole.

"It's not time to wake up!"
said Old Groundhog.

"Come back in the spring!"
called Brownie Bear.

"Go away!"
shouted Mrs. Shrew.

"What a bunch of sleepyheads!" said Reddy Cardinal.
"No one will wake up."

Then Reddy tapped at the door of the hollow tree. "It's Christmas," he said once more. "Come and see the snow."

The door suddenly flew open and three little raccoon heads popped out. "What's snow?" cried Fil, Bert, and Hazel.

The little raccoons had never seen snow before. They were soon tumbling and laughing and sliding and shouting. They made so much noise that they woke up Snowshoe Hare, who was sleeping under the ground.

Snowshoe hopped out of bed as soon as he knew it was Christmas. Off he went with his sled to wake up the other animals.

Soon a merry bunch of animals arrived at Brownie's door. "Merry Christmas!" they cried, and in they went.

"Come on in, Reddy!" said Snowshoe. "You are our special guest."

What a party they had that day!

Brownie made a cozy fire and Old Groundhog served his snappy root beer. Mrs. Shrew lit the candles on the Christmas tree. Tubby Mole filled the table with delicious treats.

Then it was time to open presents.

There were toys for the Raccoon children and a new basket for Mrs. Shrew. There were mittens for Old Groundhog and a jar of blackberry jam for Tubby. Snowshoe received a handsome new box from Fil, Bert, and Hazel. Brownie's present was a picture for his wall. Even Reddy received a present—a bright green scarf!

"I made up a song," said Brownie Bear after all the presents were unwrapped. "I thought of the words just before I went to sleep last fall."

"Oh, sing it!" cried Snowshoe. And so Brownie did. It went like this:

"Wake me up!
Wake me up!
Don't let me sleep till May,
Oh, what fun
It is to be
Together on Christmas day!"

When Brownie finished, all of the animals cheered. And Mrs. Shrew said that it was the very best Christmas she had ever had—even though it was only the first!